The Nutmeg Adventure

The Nutmeg Adventure

By
Lisa A. Reinhard

Illustrated by
Barbara Leonard Gibson

The Colonial Williamsburg Foundation
Williamsburg, Virginia

© 1994 by The Colonial Williamsburg Foundation   Printed in Hong Kong   ISBN 0-87935-099-7

It was a sunny summer day.

The bees hummed all around.

Young Jonah Sims leaned on his hoe

And listened to their sound.

He'd stopped his weeding long enough

To look up at the sky

And pick some shapes out of the clouds

As they went floating by.

A pig was starting to appear

With curly tail and all,

When Jonah heard the back door slam

And then his mother's call.

"Jonah Sims! Where are you, Son?

I need to ask a favor.

While baking, I've run out of spice—

My food will have no flavor!"

"Would you run down to Prentis Store
And buy some things for me?
Cinnamon and poppy seeds,
And nutmegs—I'll need three."

Jonah took his mother's list

And put the hoe away,

Glad to have a break from weeds

On such a lovely day.

He ran down Duke of Gloucester Street

And into Prentis Store,

Stacked from the floorboards to the roof

With everything and more!

It always smelled so wonderful,

Like leather, wax, and wood,

Like herbs and tea, and balls of soap,

And candied nuts, so good!

Jonah got the seasonings
His mother sent him for,
And with a final goodbye sniff
He headed out the door.

He put the seeds and cinnamon

Down in his pocket deep,

And jumped down all three steps at once

In one tremendous leap!

He strolled along and hummed a tune
He'd heard his father play,
When something shiny caught his eye.
He walked to where it lay.

"It's just a button," Jonah thought
When he'd bent down to see.
"I'd hoped it was a penny,
And I'd spend it all on me!"

"Oh well. At least there's cake tonight,

And bread baked to a turn,

And rolls for breakfast, with sweet milk,

And butter from the churn."

His head was filled with happy thoughts

About his mother's cooking.

He wandered out into the street

And didn't think of looking.

Around the corner came a horse

That ran as fast as lightning!

Jonah nearly got run down!

It was very frightening!

Jonah fell upon the ground

To get out of the way.

"Watch out! Watch out!" came a shout.

"My horse has run away!"

The horse and owner thundered past

As Jonah brushed off dirt.

He checked himself from top to toe

And found he wasn't hurt.

He sat a minute on a stump

To let his heart slow down.

He reached down in his pocket

And then began to frown.

His fingers felt a ragged hole

He hadn't known was there.

His mother's special spices

Were scattered everywhere!

The paper twist of poppy seeds

Was lying in the street.

The wooden curls of cinnamon

Were scattered 'round his feet.

He couldn't see the nutmegs though
As he looked all around.
"Oh, bother!" cried poor Jonah Sims,
His eyes glued to the ground.

He checked his pocket just in case

He'd any luck at all,

And felt two nutmegs nestled there

Hard and round and small.

Jonah searched both high and low

For nutmeg number three.

At last he saw where it had rolled.

It lay beside a tree.

While Jonah's search was going on

A goose had waddled by,

And at that self-same instant

The nutmeg caught its eye!

As quick as thought, it snapped it up,

And held it in its beak!

"Come back, you thief!" poor Jonah cried.

His voice rose to a squeak.

The goose began to run away
With Jonah giving chase.
He chased it up, he chased it down,
And all around the place!

He finally took a flying leap

To grab it by the wing.

The goose began to flap about

And squawk like anything!

But when it opened up its beak

The nutmeg dropped right out.

Jonah grabbed and held it tight,

And gave a happy shout.

Then Jonah ran directly home

As quick as he knew how.

His mother's hands were on her hips.

A frown was on her brow.

But when she saw his dusty clothes,

She knew he'd had some trouble.

Her anger melted like the snow.

It vanished like a bubble.

"What happened to you, Son?" she cried.

"You took so very long.

I thought you'd dawdled on the way.

I see that I was wrong."

So Jonah told the story

Of the horse and of the dirt.

"Well, goodness me!" his mother said,

"I'm glad that you weren't hurt!"

But when he told her of the goose,

She couldn't hide her smile.

"Oh, Jonah, dear," his mother said,

"That really was a trial!"

And Jonah got his feelings hurt.

For a second he felt daft,

But when he saw the truth of it,

They both sat down and laughed.

They laughed again at supper

When his father heard the tale.

"Well done, my son!" his father said.

"I knew you could not fail."

They had baked custard for dessert,

So smooth, so gold, so sweet.

With nutmeg grated on the top,

It really was a treat!

His father played the fiddle

When they finished up their meal.

And he wrote a tune for Jonah

Called "The Goose and Nutmeg Reel"!

To Ron and Mary Jean
for believing